Writing Builders

Neil and Nan Build

NARRATIVE NONFICTION

by Andrea Pelleschi
illustrated by Yu-Mei Han

Content Consultant
Jan Lacina, Ph.D.
College of Education
Texas Christian University

NORWOOD HOUSE PRESS
CHICAGO, ILLINOIS

Norwood House Press
P.O. Box 316598
Chicago, Illinois 60631
For information regarding Norwood House Press, please visit
our website at:
www.norwoodhousepress.com or call 866-565-2900.

Editor: Melissa York
Designer: Craig Hinton
Project Management: Red Line Editorial

Library of Congress Cataloging-in-Publication Data
Pelleschi, Andrea, 1962-
  Neil and Nan build narrative nonfiction / by Andrea Pelleschi ;
illustrated by Yu-Mei Han.
      pages cm. -- (Writing builders)
  Includes bibliographical references.
  Summary: "Neil and Nan write a nonfiction narrative about
roller coaster rides at a local amusement park. Their article
includes facts and pictures about the best rides. Additional
concepts include: hooks, sensory details, and main ideas.
Activities in the back help the reader write their own narrative
nonfiction"--Provided by publisher.
  ISBN 978-1-59953-586-9 (library edition : alk. paper)
  ISBN 978-1-60357-566-9 (ebook)
  1. Reportage literature--Authorship--Juvenile literature. 2.
Creative nonfiction--Authorship--Juvenile literature. I. Han, Yu-
Mei illustrator. II. Title.
  PN3377.5.R45P45 2013
  372.62'3--dc23
                                        2013010265

Words in **black bold** are defined in the glossary.

I Like Writing Narrative Nonfiction

At first, I wasn't sure I liked **narrative** nonfiction. Usually I like stories because they are exciting. Narrative nonfiction is like a story, but everything you write actually happened.

I have so many ideas for narrative nonfiction. I could write about my really cool grandmother, Nana Trixie. Or I could write about my favorite scientist, Isaac Newton. Or I could write about something that happened to me, like I did here.

The best way to make narrative nonfiction exciting is to write it like a story, from beginning to end. Stories have lots of interesting facts. They also describe **sensory details**, like how things sound, look, smell, taste, or feel. If I do all these things, people should really enjoy reading my story. Don't you think it would be fun to write about something that really happened?

By Neil, age 10

"What should we write for our narrative nonfiction assignment? We need an exciting story," said Nan.

"I don't know. I'm stuck!" said Neil.

"Stuck on what?" asked Mrs. Thompson, Neil's mother, as she entered the room. She had a plate of cookies and her newspaper.

"Our narrative nonfiction assignment," explained Neil. "We have to pick a **topic** and then write a true story about it."

"It's supposed to be about somewhere fun we've been," added Nan.

"Well, where have you enjoyed going in the past?" asked Mrs. Thompson.

Neil and Nan each grabbed a cookie and munched as they thought about it.

"I like exploring caves," said Nan. "We went to one on vacation, and it was fun!"

"I'd rather write about amusement parks," said Neil. "We went to Piney Woods Park for a school field trip last month."

"Why don't you make a list of things you've seen and done at both places," suggested Mrs. Thompson.

Caves
- Very dark—you need a flashlight
- Bats hang from the ceiling
- Long tunnels
- Weird shapes in the rocks

Piney Woods Park
- Exciting rides like roller coasters
- Slow rides
- Ringtoss and dart games
- Yummy food
- Dancing shows
- Lots of ice cream
- Ferris wheel

"Amusement parks sounds good," said Nan. "I love Piney Woods too!"

Neil got up and fished around in his backpack for a moment. "Ta-da!" he exclaimed, waving a pamphlet. "I found the Piney Woods brochure. This will help us remember details about the park."

"Great idea," said Mrs. Thompson. "Now, try grouping similar items together. That will help you organize your thoughts."

Neil and Nan took turns making groups.

Rides	Food	Games	Shows
roller-coasters	yummy food	ringtoss	dancing
slow rides	ice cream	darts	
spinning rides			

"Maybe we should narrow down our topic to rides at Piney Woods," said Neil. "It seems to be what we like the most."

"There are a lot of rides at the park," said Mrs. Thompson, looking over Neil and Nan's shoulders at the pamphlet. "Maybe you should pick one type."

"I like the roller coasters best," said Nan.

"Me too," said Neil. "Roller coasters it is."

"What next?" asked Mrs. Thompson.

"We need to fill out our **graphic organizer**," said Nan. "The beginning, the middle, and the end."

"Ugh," said Neil, slumping in his chair. "Writing the beginning is the hard part."

"I think I can help." Mrs. Thompson opened her newspaper. "You should start your narrative nonfiction with a **hook**. A hook is a funny story, a question, or an interesting fact. It makes your readers want to keep reading. Like this newspaper headline."

Is There a Sea Monster in the James River?

"That's a good opening," said Neil. "It really makes me want to keep reading."

Mrs. Thompson pointed to the Piney Woods pamphlet. "Maybe you can get some ideas for your own hook from this."

"This could be our hook," said Nan. She wrote for a minute and showed it to Neil.

GRAPHIC ORGANIZER

Beginning
The Dragon is our favorite coaster at Piney Woods Park.

"It's okay," said Neil, "but it seems a little boring. How about this?" He grabbed a blank sheet of paper and started writing.

Have you ever wanted to ride a dragon?

"I like it," said Nan. She gave Neil a high five. "We have our hook."

The two of them wrote the rest of the introduction and showed it to Mrs. Thompson.

Have you ever wanted to ride a dragon? On our field trip to Piney Woods Park, we did! A roller coaster called the Dragon just opened there. It's our new favorite ride.

"Looks good," said Mrs. Thompson. "You should fill out the rest of your graphic organizer next."

Neil and Nan got to work.

GRAPHIC ORGANIZER

Beginning

The Dragon is our favorite coaster at Piney Woods Park.

Middle Idea One

We rode three other coasters at Piney Woods on our field trip.

Middle Idea Two

The Gale Force is wooden and twists and turns.

Middle Idea Three

The Red Rocket shoots up fast to the top of the hill, but you have to be tall enough to ride it. Nan was too short!

Middle Idea Four

Everyone can ride the rickety coaster, but you feel like you're flying off the side of the hill.

End

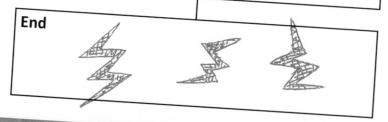

Neil started doodling under "end" because he wasn't sure what to put there yet.

"Well, let's write out the middle part in complete sentences," said Nan. "We can work on the end later."

Besides the Dragon, we rode three more coasters. First, we rode the Gale Force. It is a wooden coaster. It has lots of twists and turns. Next, Neil rode the Red Rocket. It shoots up really fast to the top of a big hill, and then it stops before roaring down the other side. However, not everyone can ride the Red Rocket. You have to be tall enough. Nan was too short, so she rode the Ferris wheel instead. The last coaster we rode is very rickety. It feels like you're going to go off the side of the hill, but you don't. Everyone can ride this one.

Nan reread their paragraph. "I think we need something between 'Not everyone can ride the Red Rocket' and 'You have to be tall enough.'"

"Oh, you mean a **linking word**," said Neil. "The word *because* would link the two sentences together."

"I like it," said Nan.

Mrs. Thompson read the paragraph. "This is a good start, but your readers will want more facts about the coasters. Can you see any places to add some?"

"We didn't name the last coaster," said Nan.

"And we never said how tall you have to be to ride the Red Rocket," added Neil.

Neil looked through the pamphlet. "It says here that the Gale Force is the longest wooden coaster in the country. That's a detail we can add."

"Let's check the Piney Woods website for more," suggested Nan. They went to use the computer in Mrs. Thompson's office. Then they came back to the sun porch and **revised** their paragraph to add the facts they found.

the longest wooden coaster in America.

Besides the Dragon, we rode three more coasters. First, we rode the Gale Force. It is ~~a wooden coaster~~. It has lots of twists and turns. Next, Neil rode the Red Rocket. It shoots up really fast to the top of a big hill, and then it stops before roaring down the other side. However, not everyone can ride the Red Rocket. ~~You have to be tall enough.~~ Nan was too short, so she rode the Ferris wheel instead. The last coaster we rode is very rickety.

because you have to be 48 inches tall.

, the Runaway Train Car,

"Very good," said Mrs. Thompson. "You know what else narrative nonfiction should have? Sensory details. What was it like to ride the coasters? How did it feel? What did you see?"

"I get it," said Nan. "We should describe the rides so our readers can pretend they were there too."

Riding the Dragon feels like flying. The wind whistles through your hair and roars loudly past your ears. If you look down, the people below look tiny. You can see the tops of their heads. Hold on tight when you turn upside down!

Neil and Nan had one more idea. They would add pictures of the coasters. They cut photos out of the pamphlet and set them aside for their final draft.

"You're almost done," said Mrs. Thompson. "Now you just have to write the end."

"I think we should talk about what the field trip and the roller coasters meant to us," said Neil.

"That will make your writing more personal," agreed Mrs. Thompson.

Nan and Neil jotted down a conclusion. Then they copied their whole story onto a clean sheet of paper and glued down pictures of the coasters.

"What do you think, Mom?" asked Neil.

Have you ever wanted to ride a dragon? On our field trip to Piney Woods Park, we did! A roller coaster called the Dragon just opened there. It's our new favorite ride.

Riding the Dragon feels like flying. The wind whistles through your hair and roars loudly past your ears. If you look down, the people below look tiny. You can see the tops of their heads. Hold on tight when you turn upside down!

Besides the Dragon, we rode three more coasters. First, we rode the Gale Force. It is the longest wooden coaster in America. It twists and turns, and you feel like you're losing your stomach. Next, Neil rode the Red Rocket. It shoots up really fast to the top of a big hill, and then it stops before roaring down the other side. However, not everyone can ride the Red Rocket because you have to be 48 inches tall. Nan was too short, so she rode the Ferris wheel instead. The last coaster we rode, the Runaway Train Car, is very rickety. It feels like you're going to go flying off the side of the hill, but you don't. Everyone can ride this one.

We had so much fun on our field trip to Piney Woods Park. Maybe we can go back when Nan is taller so she can ride the Red Rocket. And maybe we'll try some other rides too!

"This is wonderful," said Mrs. Thompson. "You even make me want to ride roller coasters, and I'm scared of heights!"

Nan and Neil laughed.

"Now all we have to do is show our narrative nonfiction to everyone else in class," said Neil.

"And go ride the Dragon again this summer!" said Nan.

Narrative nonfiction tells a story that is true. Like fiction, it is filled with interesting people, fascinating locations, and exciting events. However, narrative nonfiction also has plenty of facts. This form of nonfiction includes biographies, historical events, eyewitness accounts, and personal stories.

To write narrative nonfiction, follow these steps:

Step 1: Choose a topic. Jot down everything you know about your topic. Do you have enough material to write an entire story about it? If not, choose another topic.

Step 2: Group related items in your list together. This will help you organize your story or decide if you need to narrow your topic. You can also map out the beginning, middle, and end of your story in a graphic organizer.

Step 3: Write an introduction. Try to come up with a hook that makes your readers want to read on. A hook could be an interesting fact, a funny story, or a question that makes your readers think.

Step 4: Write the narrative. This is the part where you tell your true story. It's best to write this part from beginning to end in chronological order. Be sure to use linking words to connect different ideas together, such as *and*, *but*, *because*, *however*, and *also*.

Step 5: Make sure to include facts such as names, dates, and measurements. This will help bring your writing to life. It will also provide more information about your topic.

Step 6: Add plenty of sensory details, such as how things look, sound, feel, smell, and taste. This will paint a picture for your readers.

Step 7: Can you add illustrations or photographs? This will make your story more interesting.

Step 8: Write the conclusion of your story. The conclusion sums up what happened in the story in a new and interesting way.

Step 9: Revise. Look over your story. Can you cut out some words? Do you need to add more information? Do you have enough details to bring the story to life? Get a friend to read your story—he or she can help you see what you have written in a new light.

Step 10: Write your final draft on a clean sheet of notebook paper or type it into the computer.

Finally, make sure to share your narrative nonfiction story with others. Did they enjoy reading it?

Glossary

graphic organizer: a visual form to help you organize your ideas.

hook: a fact, quote, question, or funny story that captures a reader's attention.

linking word: a word that connects ideas together, such as *also*, *another*, *but*, and *because*.

narrative: a story or a sequence of events in the order in which they happened.

revised: took a second (or third!) look at your story to make your writing better.

sensory details: telling about how something in the story looks, sounds, feels, smells, and tastes.

topic: the main area of interest in your story.

For More Information

Books

Fandel, Jennifer. *Picture Yourself Writing Nonfiction: Using Photos to Inspire Writing*. Mankato, MN: Capstone, 2012.

MacLachlan, Patricia. *Word After Word After Word*. New York: Katherine Tegen Books, 2010.

Websites

Time for Kids A+ Papers
http://www.timeforkids.com/homework-helper/a-plus-papers
This website explains how to write many kinds of nonfiction.

Editing and Proofreading Checklist
http://planningwithkids.com/wp-content/2012/06/PWK-Editing-and-Proof-Reading.pdf
This checklist will help you revise and improve your writing.

About the Author

Andrea Pelleschi lives in Cincinnati, Ohio, with her cat, Ella. However, unlike her namesake, Cinderella, Ella never does any chores.